Glamourpuss

by Sarah Weeks

Pictures by David Small

SARDINES

SCHOLASTIC PRESS · NEW YORK

For my favorite cat lover, Kimberley Montgomery ~ S. W.

To Lily, Edison, and Oskar ~ D. S.

Text copyright © 2015 by Sarah Weeks
Illustrations copyright © 2015 by David Small

Library of Congress Control Number: 2014942281

ISBN 978-0-545-60954-8

10 9 8 7 6 5 4 3 2 1   15 16 17 18 19
Printed in China   38
First printing, February 2015

The text type was set in Pike.
The artwork was created with ink, watercolor, pastel, and collage.
Book design by David Saylor and Charles Kreloff

Once upon a pillow sat a glamorous cat named **Glamourpuss.**

Glamourpuss lived with Mr. and Mrs. Highhorsen
in a giant mansion on the top of a hill . . .

. . . where they were waited on
hand and foot by a pair of devoted
servants named Gustav and Rosalie.

The Highhorsens were gazillionaires. Having no children, they focused all their attention on Glamourpuss, showering her with expensive gifts and unbridled affection. She had her own room . . .

. . . and her own place at the dinner table. She even had a necklace made out of real diamonds.

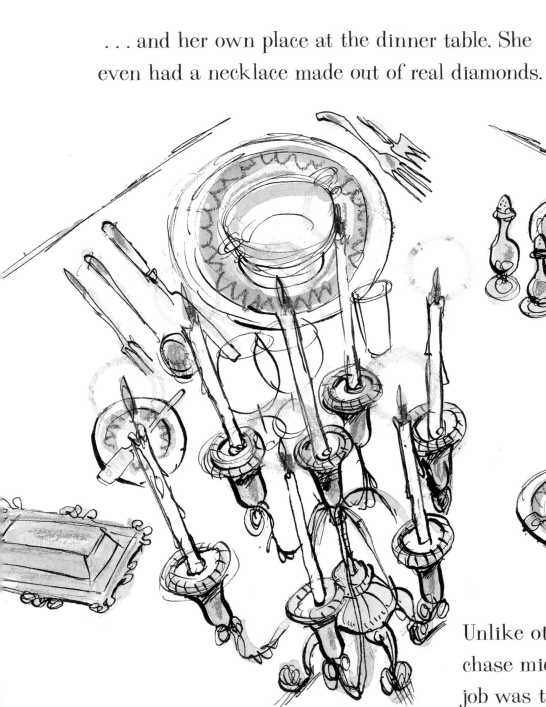

Unlike other cats, Glamourpuss wasn't expected to chase mice or rid the closets of moths. Her one and only job was to be glamorous, and she was very good at it.

Glamourpuss didn't go down stairs — she *descended*.

She didn't lie down — she *reclined*.

She didn't stretch — she *extended*.

And, because she understood that less is sometimes more, instead of saying "me-ow" like an ordinary cat, she shortened it to just . . .

Glamourpuss enjoyed living in the lap of luxury. She had everything a cat could possibly want. The Highhorsens had only to ring a little silver bell, and Gustav and Rosalie came running.

After a delicious snack, Glamourpuss would practice being glamorous. "Mirror, mirror, on the wall, who is the most glamorous of all?" she wondered, but of course the answer was obvious . . .

ME!

One day Glamourpuss was fine-tuning some
of her favorite expressions . . .

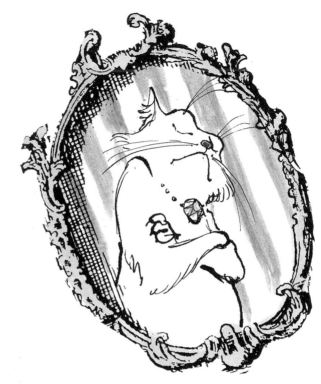

haughty disdain

slightly amused

terribly bored

. . . when **the doorbell rang.**
Mr. Highhorsen's sister, Eugenia, had come
all the way from Houston, Texas.

It appeared she was planning
to stay a while.
  And she had not come alone.

Glamourpuss took an instant dislike to Bluebelle. Her tacky wardrobe and wagging tail were reason enough to shun her, but to make matters worse . . .

Bluebelle did *tricks*.

"*First rate!*"
boomed Mr. Highhorsen.

"*Adorable!*"
squealed Mrs. Highhorsen.

"Have y'all ever seen anything more precious in your
entire life?" drawled Eugenia. "Why, couldn't you just
eat her up with a spoon?"

Absolutely, thought
Glamourpuss, and she added
a new expression to her
repertoire: *utter disgust.*

Later, when no one was looking, Glamourpuss decided to show Bluebelle a little trick of her own. She *descended* and *reclined* and then, at just the right moment, she *extended.*

Glamourpuss hoped Bluebelle would get the message and stop trying to steal her thunder, but the next day there she was again, parading around the house in another ridiculous outfit.

CLAP
CLAAYUPP
CLAP CLAP
CLAP
CLAP

CLAP

CLAP CLAP
CLAP

Then, right when Glamourpuss thought things couldn't get any worse, they did.

"Have y'all ever seen anything more *glamorous* in your life?" gushed Eugenia.

Glamourpuss couldn't believe her ears. How could *anyone* think Bluebelle was more glamorous than she was? It was preposterous! Outrageous! Absurd!

Yet, deep down inside, Glamourpuss was beginning
to worry it might actually be true.

Later that day, while everyone else was taking a nap, Glamourpuss borrowed one of Bluebelle's outfits.

"Mirror, mirror, on the wall, who is the most glamorous of all?" she wondered.

This time the answer was less obvious.

Me?

At dinner, Glamourpuss only picked at her food. Afterward, when everyone retired to the conservatory to watch Bluebelle perform a new trick, Glamourpuss slunk upstairs to lick her wounds.

The next day Glamourpuss overslept. By the time she woke up, everyone had gone out. *Nobody cares about me anymore*, she thought sadly.

Her pity party was interrupted by a strange noise coming from the guest room.

When Glamourpuss went to investigate,
she couldn't believe what she saw!

"*Bad dog!*" scolded Eugenia when she discovered what Bluebelle had done.

At first Glamourpuss was elated. Bluebelle would have a hard time stealing her thunder now that she'd chewed up all her fancy clothes.

But later, when she caught Bluebelle doing a little practicing of her own, Glamourpuss realized she'd made a terrible mistake. Bluebelle had chewed up her clothes because she despised them!

Who could blame her? The poor thing had been trapped in a nightmare of hoopskirts and fruit-covered turbans, when all she really wanted was to be glamorous, like . . .

Over the next few days Glamourpuss worked tirelessly with Bluebelle, teaching her everything she knew about being glamorous.

Bluebelle was a quick study. She mastered *descending, reclining,* and *extending* in no time flat.

True, she sometimes needed to be reminded that tail wagging is undignified . . .

. . . but it was Bluebelle herself who came up with the idea of shortening "bow-wow" to the much more glamorous . . .

Mr. and Mrs. Highhorsen were very proud of the way Glamourpuss had taken Bluebelle under her wing. Eugenia wasn't happy about it at first, but eventually she learned to accept Bluebelle's true nature.

As for Glamourpuss, she learned an important lesson too. When it comes to being glamorous, less is sometimes more, but when it comes to having friends . . .

. . . you can never have too many.